D0131240

Finley Flowers

Room to Bloom

BY JESSICA YOUNG

ILLUSTRATED BY JESSICA SECHERET

PICTURE WINDOW BOOKS
a capstone imprint

Finley Flowers is published by Picture Window Books
A Capstone imprint
1710 Roe Crest Drive
North Mankato, Minnesota 56003
www.mycapstone.com

Text © 2018 Jessica Young
Illustrations © 2018 Picture Window Books

All rights reserved. No part of this publication may be reproduced in whole
or in part, or stored in a retrieval system, or transmitted in any form or by
any means, electronic, mechanical, photocopying, recording, or otherwise,
without written permission of the publisher.

Library of Congress Cataloging-in-Publication Data is available
on the Library of Congress website.

ISBN: 978-1-4795-9806-9 (hardcover)
ISBN: 978-1-4795-9810-6 (paper-over-board)
ISBN: 978-1-4795-9826-7 (eBook PDF)
ISBN: 978-1-4795-9830-4 (reflowable epub)

Summary: Finley's class is building a class garden, but when Finley's crops
fail to sprout, she and her friends start to wonder if their seeds are duds.

Editor: Alison Deering
Designer: Lori Bye

Vector Images: Shutterstock ©

Printed and bound in the USA.
010400F17

For Lana, Susannah, and everyone
who likes to garden

TABLE OF CONTENTS

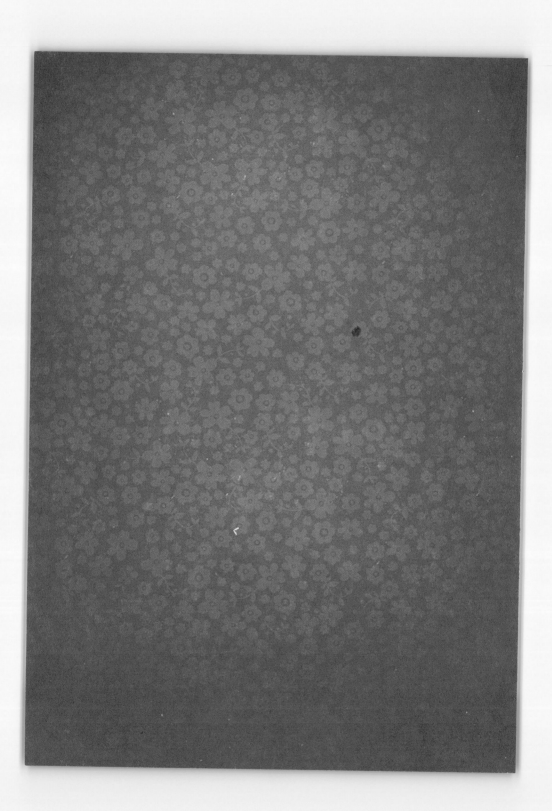

Chapter 1

A FRESH IDEA

As Finley's fourth-grade class filed in from recess, their teacher took her place at the front of the room. Ms. Bird always had interesting things to share, but Finley had a feeling something special was coming. She could tell by the way her teacher's eyes lit up as she rang the chime.

When all the students had taken their seats, Ms. Bird unrolled a big scroll of paper and held it up. "I got this new poster for our classroom," she said. "Will someone please read it for us?"

Finley raised her hand.

Ms. Bird smiled. "Finley?"

"The best way to find yourself is to lose yourself
in the service of others," Finley read. "By Gandhi."

"Thank you," Ms. Bird said. "Who has an idea about what that means?"

Henry Lin, Finley's best friend, raised his hand. "I don't know," he answered, "but if you're lost, the best way to find yourself is a map. Or a compass. Or a GPS."

Ms. Bird laughed. "Maps are handy," she agreed, "and compasses and GPSs too. Does anyone else have something to add?"

The class was silent.

How can the best way to find yourself be to lose yourself? Finley wondered.

She was about to ask when Ms. Bird turned around and started erasing yesterday's homework from the board.

"Keep thinking about it," the teacher said over her shoulder. "You might get an idea as you're working on our next project." Turning back to the board, she wrote the words *SERVICE PROJECT* in big letters. "Each spring, the fourth graders plan and complete a service project to better-ify our school and community. This year it's *your* turn."

"Last year, Ms. Silva's class had a litter cleanup day at the park," Henry said.

Ms. Bird nodded. "That's right. They even raised money to buy some extra trash cans so there would be more places to throw garbage away."

Olivia Snotham made a face. "Ew," she whispered to Finley. "I don't want to spend the day picking up other people's trash."

Finley smiled at her friend and shrugged. "At least we'd get to be outside."

"There are so many ways to make a difference," Ms. Bird continued. "Today we'll brainstorm ideas together, and tomorrow we'll vote to choose a project. Remember that whatever we pick should be something that makes our school or community better. Any thoughts or questions?"

Henry raised his hand. "Is it almost time for lunch?"

Ms. Bird glanced at the clock and smiled. "Yes, Henry, it is. Pack up your things, everyone, and be ready to brainstorm when you get back."

Finley and her friends filed down the hall to the cafeteria.

"I'll save you a spot," Olivia said. "I packed my lunch today."

"Great!" Henry said as he and Finley headed to get their trays.

Finley went through the line and joined Olivia at a corner table. She plunked her tray down and examined her lunch. "I like peas, but not these," she said, smushing one on the tip of her fork and examining it.

"Maybe because they're not green," Olivia said. "And they're all mushy."

"I like them fresh, like the ones we grow in my mom's garden," Henry said, taking a seat beside Finley.

"Why can't they make them like that?" Olivia asked.

"Because those come from a can," Henry said, pointing to Finley's plate.

Olivia unwrapped her sandwich. "Well, why don't they get fresh ones?"

Henry shrugged. "You got me. The carrots are soggy too. They taste like a sponge."

Finley ate her spaghetti, then took her tray to the trash. On the way, she glanced around the room. It was the same at every table — no one had touched their vegetables.

What a waste, she thought. *They might as well not serve them at all.*

As she stood there beside the garbage can, Finley felt an idea seed starting to sprout. She dumped her trash and ran back to the table. "Hey," she said to Henry, "got a pencil?"

"Always." Henry fished one out of his pocket.

Finley took it and started scribbling notes on a napkin.

"What are you doing?" Olivia asked, peering over Finley's shoulder.

"Brainstorming," Finley said. "Hold on a sec." She finished what she was writing and handed the pencil back.

"What's that about?" Henry asked, pointing to the napkin. "Or is it top secret?"

Finley laughed. "It's not top secret — it's an idea for our service project."

"Well, out with it!" Henry said. "What's growing in your idea garden?"

Finley grinned. "Carrots."

Henry raised an eyebrow. "Carrots? As in your favorite vegetable?"

Finley nodded. "And peas and lettuce and tomatoes and spinach."

Henry looked confused. "Oookay . . ."

Finley pointed to Henry's mushy peas. "What if we didn't *have* to eat soggy veggies? Maybe we could grow our own!"

"At school?" Olivia asked, wrinkling her brow.

Finley shrugged. "Why not? It'd be fun."

"Gardening is a lot of work," Henry said. "My mom weeds and waters our garden practically every day."

"We would have a lot of people to share the work," Olivia pointed out.

"Yep," Finley said. "We'd have the whole class."

"True," Henry agreed. "Maybe you should bring it up in class brainstorming and see what Ms. Bird says."

"I will," Finley said. "A class garden could be the most Fin-tastic service project ever!"

Chapter 2

VOTE FOR VEGGIES

After lunch, Ms. Bird erased the board. "Who's ready to brainstorm?" she asked. "Remember, we need to identify a problem or need in our community and come up with a way to help. Let's list some ideas."

Finley and several other students raised their hands.

Ms. Bird grabbed a marker from the mug on her desk and pointed to Finley's friend Lia. "Yes, Lia?"

"We could go to the animal shelter and play with dogs and cats," Lia suggested. "That helps them get used to being around people before they're adopted."

"Great idea," Ms. Bird said, writing *Animal Shelter* on the board. "That would involve a field trip, but it might be possible." She pointed to Amelia next.

"We could do a food drive," Amelia said, "and collect food for people who need it."

"Or a book drive for kids who need books," Kate added.

Ms. Bird wrote *Food Drive* and *Book Drive* on the board. "There are lots of organizations that collect food and books and give them to people in need," she said, turning back to the class. "What's your idea, Will?"

"We could go to an assisted living center and do something nice for senior citizens," Will said. "My grandpa lives in one. He loves when I visit."

"Good thinking," Ms. Bird said. "Giving people our time is just as important as donating money or things." She added *Assisted Living Visit* to the list, then nodded in Finley's direction. "Finley?"

"We could plant a school garden," Finley said, "and grow fresh vegetables for the cafeteria."

"That's an interesting idea," Ms. Bird said. "Tell me more."

"I noticed at lunch that most kids throw away their veggies," Finley continued. "I think it's because the vegetables don't really taste like vegetables. A garden would fix that. We could feed the whole school!"

Ms. Bird smiled. "We might not have enough vegetables to feed *everyone*," she said. "But we could start with our class. If it goes well, other classes might want to build their own gardens." She paused with the marker in her hand. "Where we would put this garden?"

"How about right there?" Finley pointed out the window. "There's plenty of room, and we could watch it grow. We could even get picnic tables or blankets and eat lunch outside."

"I'd have to get permission from Principal Small, but that just might work." Ms. Bird wrote *Class Garden/Outdoor Classroom* on the board. "Any other thoughts or questions?"

Will raised his hand. "What does outdoor classroom mean?"

"Some schools have an outdoor space where classes can do experiments and lessons or just go out and read," Ms. Bird explained.

"Class on the grass!" Henry blurted out.

Lia's eyes lit up. "You mean school would be outside?"

Ms. Bird nodded. "Not all the time, but sometimes, yes." She glanced around the room. "Does anyone else have another service project idea to share?"

No one raised a hand.

"We've got quite a list," Ms. Bird said. "I'll leave it up on the board so you can think about it before we vote tomorrow. These are all wonderful ideas — it's going to be difficult to choose just one."

"I know what I'm choosing," Henry whispered to Finley. "It starts with *G* and ends with *N*."

"We have half an hour before we go to P.E.," Ms. Bird continued. "You can use it to research your projects or make signs to get people to vote for them."

Finley turned to Henry. "Want to help me make some signs?"

"Sure," Henry said. "*Sign* me up!"

"Can I help?" Olivia asked. "I'm all for a class garden. It would make our view a lot prettier."

"Of course," Finley said. "First we need a good slogan — something catchy that'll make everyone want to vote for our idea."

"Vote for veggies!" Henry said.

Finley laughed. "That has a nice ring to it. And we could draw veggies on the signs."

"Maybe each sign could feature a different vegetable and a different saying," Olivia suggested.

"Class garden — you can't *beet* it!" Henry said, grinning.

"*Lettuce* plant lettuce!" Olivia exclaimed.

"*Peas* and love!" Finley added. "Let's get *growing*!"

"Ooh," Olivia said. "I like that one."

Finley grabbed a stack of large, white paper and some markers from the craft table, and the three friends got to work.

"What are you drawing?" Henry asked as Finley started to sketch.

"My favorite vegetable," Finley said. She finished drawing a smiling cartoon carrot, then wrote *SHOW YOU CARE — PLANT A CAR-ROT!* in bubble letters across the top of her paper.

"Ha! Nice one." Henry wrote *CLASS GARDEN — A BERRY GOOD IDEA* and drew a giant strawberry on his sign.

By the end of class, Finley, Henry, and Olivia had finished six signs. At recess they took a roll of masking tape and posted the signs around the classroom and in the hall.

"There," Finley said, taping the last one to the bulletin board. "The signs are up. Now let's just hope people will vote for veggies!"

Chapter 3

GREEN THUMB

"I talked with my mom about your garden idea," Henry said as he and Finley walked into class the next morning. "She told me to give you this." He pulled a *Good Growing* magazine out of his backpack.

"Wow, thanks," Finley said, studying the huge vegetable garden on the cover.

"One of the articles is about school gardens around the world," Henry said. "Some of them even donate part of what they grow to local food banks and shelters."

"That would be great," Olivia said, peering over Finley's shoulder. "Then we could do two service projects at once."

"We might not have enough veggies to donate at the beginning," Henry said. "But we could start small and expand the garden as we go."

"Sounds good," Finley said. "I'm all for sharing." She flipped through the magazine. "Did you see some of these? One of them even has a pizza garden with an outdoor pizza oven!"

Lia bounded over to look. "Ooh! I want to grow pizza!"

Henry laughed. "That *would* be awesome! I don't think we can grow pizza, but we *can* grow most of the ingredients we need to make it. Tomatoes, basil, garlic . . ."

"Cheese!" Will chimed in.

"Ha," Henry grinned. "Cheese doesn't grow on trees. But a school in this magazine grows wheat to make dough for pizza crust. They use a cool bicycle-powered mill to grind the wheat into flour."

"Whoa," Kate said. "If we had one of those, every day could be pizza day!"

Henry nodded. "And we could grow tons of stuff to put on our pizzas too. Peppers, mushrooms, spinach. . . . I could go for some pizza right now!"

"Mmm," Finley said. "Make mine double olives, extra cheese!"

"Okay, class, let's get started," Ms. Bird said as she rang the chime. "We'll go over our math problems in a bit, but first it's time to vote on our service project." She pointed to the ideas they'd listed the day before. "Does anyone have anything to add before we vote?"

Lia put up her hand.

"Lia?"

"Can I take my idea off the list? I like Finley's better. Field trips are fun, but an outdoor classroom is like having a field trip every day."

"Sure," said Ms. Bird, erasing *Animal Shelter* from the list. "There are still a lot of great ideas to choose from. Anything else before we begin?"

The room was quiet.

"Okay," Ms. Bird said, "then let's vote." She walked around the class, passing out small strips of paper. "Please write down the idea you want to vote for, then fold your paper in half and put it in the basket on my desk."

As Finley studied the ideas on the board, her stomach sank. *Ms. Bird is right*, she thought. *All of the ideas are great. But I really want a garden.*

Henry leaned over in his seat. "Vote for veggies," he whispered.

Finley grinned at him and wrote *Class Garden* on her paper. She folded it twice, walked over to Ms. Bird's desk, and dropped it in the basket. Then she crossed her fingers and waited.

When all of the papers had been turned in, Ms. Bird read them one by one and made tally marks on the board.

Finley couldn't watch. She took out her sketchbook and started drawing a plant. Its leaves stretched toward the top of the page, and its roots branched out like upside-down trees at the bottom.

"Well, that settles it," Ms. Bird said. "The votes have been counted, and our official service project is . . ."

Finley's heart beat faster as Ms. Bird paused.

"A class garden!" Ms. Bird smiled. "Thanks to everyone for contributing your ideas and your votes."

"Yes!" Henry gave Finley a fist bump.

"First, Principal Small will have to approve our project," Ms. Bird continued. "I'll ask her about it today, and hopefully, we'll hear back by Monday. Then we'll get to work. And speaking of work . . . please take out your math problems."

"Congratulations on the garden," Will told Finley as they got out their books. "I just hope it grows."

"Of course it'll grow," Finley said. "Why wouldn't it?"

"Have you ever tried to grow anything?" Will asked. "It's not as easy as it looks."

"Don't worry," Finley told him. "We'll have the most Fin-tastic garden ever — or my last name isn't Flowers!"

* * *

"We're going to grow a garden for our service project at school," Finley announced that night at dinner. "It was my idea, and the class voted for it."

"Good luck with that," her older brother, Zack, said, twirling spaghetti around his fork.

Finley glared. "What's that supposed to mean?"

"Just that this family isn't known for gardening skills," Zack said. "Every time we get a potted plant, it winds up crispy and brown."

"What about the one with red flowers Mom puts out every winter?" Finley asked. "We've had it for years."

"That's because it's plastic," Zack said, reaching for the garlic bread.

"We're great at growing dandelions," Finley's little sister, Evie, chimed in.

"Those don't count," Zack said. "Dandelions are weeds."

Evie shrugged. "I don't care — I think they're pretty."

"Zack is right," Mom said matter-of-factly. "Your dad and I aren't so good at growing things."

Dad nodded. "I don't exactly have a green thumb."

"Well, *I* do," Finley said, straightening in her chair.

Mom smiled. "Good. I think a school garden is a great idea. Maybe you can share some tips with us."

Finley grinned. "Maybe I'll even share my veggies."

Zack is wrong, she thought. *I'm going to be a Fin-tastic gardener.*

Chapter 4

PLAN TO PLANT

On Monday morning when Finley got to class, the desks were pushed together into small groups. As Finley took her seat with Henry and Olivia, Ms. Bird rang the chime.

"Principal Small approved our service project," she announced. "Who's ready to create a garden?"

"MEEEEEE!" everyone yelled.

"Excellent." Ms. Bird smiled. "First, you'll be working in groups to plan the garden and build frames for the garden beds. Then we'll plant our seeds. I'm hoping we can throw a harvest party when the first crops are ready to pick."

"Where will we get the soil?" Finley asked.

"One of our Glendale Elementary parents owns a landscaping company," Ms. Bird said. "Over the weekend, she dropped off some wood to make our frames. She'll be coming back to deliver soil and straw we can use for mulch."

Olivia raised her hand. "What's mulch?"

"Mulch is what you spread on top of your garden," Ms. Bird explained. "It keeps moisture in the soil and protects plants from extreme temperatures. It also prevents weeds from growing. There are a lot of different types of mulch, but straw is one of the best for veggie gardens."

"I love straw," Henry whispered to Finley. "Maybe we'll have extra so we can jump in it!"

"We're going to need gardening tools," Ms. Bird continued. "Shovels, rakes, watering cans, and trowels. We'll buy some to keep at school, but it would be great if you could also bring some from home."

"I'll ask my mom if I can borrow ours," Henry offered. "We've got tons of gardening tools."

"Thank you, Henry," Ms. Bird said. "Now, I need a person from each group to come get garden journals." She pointed to the stack on her desk. "We'll use these to plan, write observations, and sketch our plants as they grow."

Finley hopped up and grabbed three journals from the pile. She handed Henry and Olivia theirs, then got busy sketching her name on the front of her own in leafy letters.

"Before we get started planning," Ms. Bird said, "let's make a list of all the things we want our garden to have or be."

"I want it to be beautiful," Olivia said, "with lots of colors."

Ms. Bird wrote *Beauty/Color* on the board. "Flowers would be beautiful," she said. "And vegetables also come in a rainbow of colors."

"The garden should be peaceful," Lia said. "With a good place to read."

"That sounds wonderful." Ms. Bird wrote *Space to Read*.

Finley thought about Henry's garden. It always smelled so good, especially after it rained. "I'd like it to smell nice," she said.

"Good idea," Ms. Bird said. "Lots of flowers and herbs smell great." She added *Good Smells* to the list.

"It would be nice to have a shady spot to sit in," Henry suggested.

"Agreed," Ms. Bird said as she wrote *Shade for Sitting*.

"Is there enough room for all this stuff?" Will asked.

"Let's find out," Ms. Bird replied. "Everyone take out a piece of graph paper, a pencil, and a ruler, and we'll start designing our garden."

"Yes!" Henry said. "I love measuring."

"Our outdoor space is thirty feet long by forty feet wide and ends just past the big maple tree." Ms. Bird drew a line at the bottom of the board. "Each square on your graph paper equals one square foot in the garden. Draw a line thirty squares long across on the bottom of your paper. Then measure forty squares up and make a big rectangle. That's what our garden space will look like."

Finley counted squares and drew the shape of the garden on her paper. Then she wrote *Class Garden* at the top in her nicest printing.

"As you think about how to divide the space, remember we talked about having veggies, herbs, and flowers, and somewhere for the class to sit." Ms. Bird pointed to the items on the board. "Any other ideas?"

"We need shade, but the vegetables will need sun," Henry said. "I know that from our garden at home."

"Good thinking," Ms. Bird said. "What else do plants need to grow?"

"Soil," Arpin said, "with lots of nutrients. We learned that last year in science."

"Uh-huh." Ms. Bird added it to the list.

"Water!" Finley said.

Ms. Bird nodded. "Right. When it doesn't rain, we'll need to water the garden. Luckily, there's a spigot on the outside wall where we can attach a hose. We'll also collect rainwater in barrels."

"How big should the garden beds be?" Finley asked.

"Good question," Ms. Bird said. "We'll have six vegetable beds — one for each group. None of the beds should be wider than four feet. Can anyone guess why?"

No one raised a hand.

"Stretch your arms out in front of you," Ms. Bird instructed. "How far can you reach?"

Henry looked thoughtful. "Maybe about two feet?" he guessed.

Ms. Bird nodded. "Mm-hmm . . ."

"If the garden beds are four feet across or less, we'll be able to reach into the middle of them to plant and pick stuff!" Finley said.

Ms. Bird smiled. "Exactly. Plus we'll build the frames for the vegetable garden beds out of wood that's been cut in four-foot lengths. Think about that as you design your garden plans. Let's take twenty minutes to sketch some ideas."

Finley studied the list on the board. She glanced out the window, then back at her page. Starting near the bottom, she drew six square garden beds. Then she added crisscrossing paths between them.

"Are those the veggie beds?" Henry asked, leaning over to look at her paper.

Finley nodded. "Now we need flowers and somewhere to sit."

Sketching the maple tree near the top of her paper, Finley left a space under it for the sitting area. Next she added a tall wooden structure covered with winding vines.

"Wow," Henry said. "That's a Fin-tastic plan! I'd like to sit under that arbor and read."

Finley nodded. "We can grow vines all over it for shade. I'm going to put the flower and herb garden next to it so we can look at the flowers and smell the herbs." She pointed to Henry's drawing. "Let's see yours."

"Mine has more space between the garden beds," Henry said, holding up his paper. "But my sitting area is smaller."

"It's awesome," Finley said. "I like how the beds fan out like spokes."

Just then Ms. Bird rang the chime. "All right, class, please finish up. If you'd like to share your design, come tape it to the board."

Finley grabbed a piece of tape from Ms. Bird's desk and stuck her drawing up beside Henry's. Once the designs had been posted, Ms. Bird gave the class some time to look them over.

"So," she said after a few minutes, "what do you think?"

"I like Henry's garden beds," Finley replied.

"I like the paths around the gardens on that one," Arpin said, pointing to Finley's.

"And I like the fancy sitting area covered with vines," Olivia added. "It's perfect for a picnic."

"But how would we build that?" Will asked.

"I'm not sure we could make the arbor right away," Ms. Bird said, "but maybe we could get parent volunteers to help build it later. Raise your hand if you want to use this one as a general plan."

A bunch of hands went up.

"Great!" Ms. Bird said. She grabbed a box from her desk and led the class toward the door. "Come on — let's get growing!"

Chapter 5

BUILD A BED

"According to our design, each group will build a garden bed in this area," Ms. Bird said once they were all outside. "First, choose a spot. Then get a tape measure and plot out a four-by-four-foot square for your group. You can use these to mark the corners." She reached into the box she'd been carrying and pulled out a wooden stake.

Ms. Bird set the box down on the grass. The groups took their tape measures and stakes and spread out on the lawn.

Finley found a spot close to the outside wall. "How about over here?"

"Looks good," Olivia said.

"Yep," Henry agreed. "It's nice and sunny and protected from the wind."

Finley pushed a stake into the ground by Henry's feet, then pulled out the tape measure. "Here," she said. "Hold that."

Henry held the end of the tape measure against the stake, and Finley measured four feet. "One side is done," she said, pushing another stake into the ground.

Finley, Henry, and Olivia measured the remaining sides and marked off their square. Then they stood back to admire their work.

"That's a king-sized bed," Henry said happily. "We'll have plenty of room to grow lots of veggies."

When the other groups had finished, Ms. Bird called the class to gather. Finley sat on the grass beside Olivia and Henry.

"Aaah!" Olivia cried, swatting at a bug.

"Don't hurt it," Henry said. "What if it's a good bug?"

"*Good* bug?" Olivia shook her head. "No such thing."

"There are lots of good bugs," Henry said. "In fact, we *need* bugs to help us grow our food."

"That's true," Ms. Bird said. "We rely on pollinators like bees, butterflies, and flies for growing cantaloupes, watermelons, kiwis, pumpkins, squash, vanilla, and chocolate — and they help with lots of other crops too."

"Chocolate?" Olivia said. "Okay, maybe pollinators are good bugs."

"What do pollinators do?" Kate asked.

"They carry pollen from one flower to another," Ms. Bird explained. "Plants give pollinators nectar and pollen for food, and pollinators help plants make seeds and grow fruit. They need each other."

Finley's eyes lit up. "Then we should plant some plants that pollinators like!"

"That's a great idea," Ms. Bird said. "But *bee*-fore we can plant, we have to build frames for our vegetable garden beds." She walked over to a pile of lumber and picked up two pieces of wood. "These cedar boards have been pre-cut and pre-drilled with holes."

Ms. Bird set the boards against the ground to form a corner. "Line up the holes in the ends of two boards, then slide one of these long, metal rods in to hold them together." She pushed the rod into the hole to demonstrate.

"That looks easy," Henry said.

"It is easy," Ms. Bird said with a smile. "Join four boards to make a square frame, and position it where

you've marked off your garden. You can remove
the stakes from the ground once you've built your
bed. When you're ready, grab your materials and get
building."

Olivia grabbed four rods. Finley and Henry
dragged four boards over to the place where they'd
marked off their garden.

Finley pushed two boards together to make a
corner so the holes lined up. Henry held them so

they wouldn't move. Then Olivia slid a rod into the
hole.

"Ta-daah!" she said. "One down!"

Olivia held the next board while Henry finished
another corner. Then it was Finley's turn. When they
were done, they examined their frame.

"Looks square," Henry said, testing one of the
corners. "And solid."

Finley waved Ms. Bird over.

"Nice work," Ms. Bird said. "You're almost ready for soil."

Olivia frowned. "Almost? This garden is a lot of work, and we haven't even planted it yet."

"Don't worry," Finley told her. "It'll be worth it."

"Follow me!" Ms. Bird called, heading over to a stack of flattened cardboard boxes. Finley, Henry, and Olivia trailed behind her.

"Use this cardboard to cover up the ground inside your frame," Ms. Bird told them. "That'll keep out the grass and weeds."

Finley, Henry, and Olivia grabbed some boxes. They laid them on the ground inside the frame, tucking in the edges.

"We're done!" Finley called to Ms. Bird. "Bring on the soil!"

"Great work!" Ms. Bird answered. "The soil will be delivered later today. Tomorrow you should come to school ready to get messy. And don't forget to bring extra shovels or trowels for digging."

* * *

When Finley got home from school, Dad was in the kitchen putting away groceries.

"Do we have a shovel I can bring to school tomorrow?" Finley asked. "Or one of those gardening trowels?"

"The shovel is in the garage," Dad said, "and the trowel should be too. Although I'll have to look for it — we haven't used it in a while."

Just then Evie skipped in from the living room. "What's for dinner?" she asked, peering into the fridge.

"Breakfast," Dad answered. "I thought I'd make pancakes."

"Woo-hoo!" Evie cheered. "Breakfast for dinner is my favorite!"

Dad finished putting the groceries away. "Come on," he said to Finley, "let's look for that trowel."

Finley followed him into the garage.

"There's the shovel," Dad said, pointing to a jumble of tools in the corner. Digging around in a big, plastic bin, he pulled out a pointed trowel. "Here." He handed it to Finley. "You're all set."

"Thanks," Finley said. She grabbed the shovel as Dad headed back inside.

"What's that for?" Evie asked, peering through the doorway.

"Our class garden," Finley answered.

"Lucky!" Evie said. "I love digging in the dirt!"

Just then, the side door swung open, and Zack walked his bike into the garage. "Hey," he said, parking it against the wall. "What's up with the shovel?"

"I'm taking it to school," Finley said. "Tomorrow we get to plant our seeds!"

Zack took off his helmet and hung it from his handlebars. "Well, when they don't grow, don't worry. We'll buy a bunch of veggies and sneak over one night to stick them in the ground."

"Thanks," Finley said, rolling her eyes. "But that won't be necessary. Our garden is going to grow great — just wait."

Chapter 6
DIG IN

The next morning when Finley and Henry got to class, they set their gardening tools by Ms. Bird's desk and ran to look out the windows. A mountain of soil sat outside.

"Whoa!" Henry said, pointing to the pile.

"It looks like our soil was delivered," Ms. Bird said. "We'd better choose some seeds." She picked up a catalog from the stack on her desk. "Look through these seed catalogs in your groups. Then cut out pictures of things you'd like to plant and use them to make a garden collage."

Ms. Bird passed out the seed catalogs and paper, and the class got to work. Finley held up a picture of towering yellow flowers. "Look at these sunflowers!"

"Oooh!" Olivia said. "We need some!"

"Don't forget carrots," Henry said, cutting out a picture.

"And zucchini," Finley added. "My dad makes the best zucchini bread."

"Hey, why was the zucchini flat?" Henry asked.

Finley shrugged. "I don't know."

"It got *squash*ed."

"Ha," Finley said. "I bet that made it grump-*pea*."

"How do you grow a chicken?" Henry asked.

"A *chicken*?" Finley made a face.

Henry grinned. "Plant an *egg*-plant."

Olivia groaned. "Enough with the *corn*-y jokes." She held up a picture of some pearly white-and-yellow corn.

Finley, Henry, and Olivia arranged all their pictures on a piece of paper and glued them in place.

"What about tomatoes?" Henry asked. "And basil and garlic? I want to have a pizza garden."

"That sounds yummy," Ms. Bird said from behind him. "But we'll have to wait to plant tomatoes. They grow best in warmer temperatures. We're going to grow early spring vegetables first."

"That's okay," Finley said. "We can make salad instead."

Once all of the groups had finished, Ms. Bird posted the garden collages on the board. "Look at those fruits and vegetables!" she said. "Some of them are summer crops — we'll plant them later in the year. I'll go ahead and buy the early spring seeds so we can get started. But first we need to prepare the garden beds."

"Time to get messy!" Finley said happily.

Ms. Bird led the class out to the garden. They gathered in front of the pile of earth.

"Whoa," Kate said. "That's a lot of dirt."

"That's a lot of *soil*," Ms. Bird corrected. "Soil is better than dirt. It's full of nutrients our plants will need. Try to spread it evenly in the raised beds. It should be at least eight inches deep so the plants' roots will have room to grow."

"How do we get the soil to our garden?" Finley asked.

Ms. Bird pointed to a row of tools that were leaning against the building. "I put out the shovels, rakes, and wheelbarrows that many of you brought from home. Please share the tools — let's start with two shovels and one wheelbarrow per group — and make sure to use them carefully."

Finley grabbed the shovel she'd brought in and handed another one to Henry. Olivia wheeled a wheelbarrow over to the pile of soil.

"Okay, team — dig in!" Finley drove her shovel into the pile.

Finley, Henry, and Olivia took turns scooping up shovelfuls of soil. They dug until they'd made a hole in the side of the mountain.

"Gardening is hard work," Olivia said, pausing to catch her breath.

Henry leaned on his shovel. "No kidding. And the wheelbarrow's only half full."

"Let's see how heavy it is." Finley lifted the handles and groaned. "Ugh! This thing weighs a ton!"

"Good luck," Will called, as he wheeled a small pile of soil toward his garden. "I'm going to dump this and come back for more."

"Maybe we should take a small load too," Henry suggested.

"Just a bit more," Finley said. "Then we'll get it done faster."

Henry and Olivia exchanged a look as they piled on more soil. Then Henry grabbed the handles and tried to push the wheelbarrow. It didn't budge.

"Yikes," he said. "I can barely lift it."

"No problem," Finley said, making a muscle. "Stand back."

She grabbed the handles and pushed with all her weight. The wheelbarrow wobbled as Finley gritted her teeth and headed for their empty garden frame.

"Careful . . . careful . . ." Henry coached, walking beside her as she teetered across the lawn.

"Don't worry," Finley told him. "I've got it!"

Will, Kate, and Lia watched as Finley struggled to steer around their garden bed. "I hope you have a license to drive that thing," Will said. "We're lucky *our* garden is the closest. We don't have far to go."

Finley glared at Will and gave the wheelbarrow an extra shove — just as the front wheel dipped into a hole in the grass.

"Aaaaah!" she shrieked as the wheelbarrow tipped.

Henry and Olivia dove to help, but it was too late. Finley fell to her knees, and the rich, brown earth spilled across the grass.

"Are you okay?" Will asked, offering a hand to help Finley up.

"I'm *fine*," Finley said, fighting back tears. She scrambled to her feet and brushed the soil off her jeans.

Olivia sighed. "Better get the shovels. This time I'll drive."

Finley, Henry, and Olivia got to work scooping up the spilled soil. Will, Kate, and Lia helped too. Then Henry and Olivia each took a wheelbarrow handle and staggered toward the garden.

When they got there, Finley grabbed the side of the wheelbarrow. "On the count of three," she said to Henry and Olivia. "One . . . two . . . three . . ."

They tipped the wheelbarrow together, and the soil slid out into the garden bed.

"Finally," Olivia said, giving Finley a limp fist bump.

"Come on," Henry said, turning the wheelbarrow around. "Let's get some more."

The class dug and dumped until the entire mountain of soil was gone. Then they raked the garden beds until they were smooth and level.

Henry grabbed a tape measure. "I'll make sure the soil is deep enough." He walked along the outside of their garden frame, stopping every few feet to measure. "Eight inches all the way around!" he announced after inspecting the last section.

"I can't wait till we get our seeds!" Finley said. "I think they're going to like their new home."

Chapter 7

READY, SET, GROW!

After two days of rain, the sun finally broke through the clouds. Ms. Bird greeted everyone when they arrived, then stood at the front of the class. "The sun is out, and it's time to plant!" she announced, holding up a packet of seeds.

"Yes!" Finley said. "I can't wait to get my hands dirty!"

"I don't want to get my hands dirty," Olivia said. "I just painted my nails last night." She pulled a pair of purple polka-dot gardening gloves out of her backpack. "Luckily, I came prepared."

Finley raised her hand. "What are we planting?" she asked.

"Let's find out," Ms. Bird said. "I need a member of each group to come up and pick a packet of seeds from my watering can. Read the back of your packet, look at the planting chart I've drawn on the board, and make a similar chart in your journal. Be sure to include today's date, the type of seeds, planting depth, seed spacing, and germination time — that's how long they take to start growing."

"I hope we get carrots," Finley said.

"I want beets," Olivia said. "They're the prettiest purple."

"I'll be happy with anything," Henry said. "I've never met a veggie I didn't like."

"This group looks ready." Ms. Bird pointed to Frances, Arpin, and Luis. "Send someone over to pick your seeds."

Luis jumped up and headed to the teacher's desk. Ms. Bird held the watering can high as Luis reached in.

"No peeking," she warned.

Luis fished around and pulled out a packet. "Beets!" he said, bounding back to his group.

"Looks like he *beet* us to the beets," Henry said.

Olivia frowned. "Those should have been mine. No one appreciates purple like I do."

"Next up, Tyra's group," Ms. Bird said.

Tyra picked a packet and held it up. "Spinach!"

Harper's group went after Tyra and got lettuce. Amelia's group picked peas.

Finley sat as straight and still as she could. *We have to be next. I need carrots.*

"Will's group," Ms. Bird said.

Will fished around in the watering can and held up a packet. "Carrots!" he said, grinning. "I love carrots!" Kate and Lia gave him a thumbs-up.

Finley slumped in her chair. "So do I."

"It's okay," Henry told her. "We'll still get to eat them."

"And last but not least, Finley's group," Ms. Bird said cheerily.

Finley shuffled to the front of the class. Then she held her breath and reached into the watering can.

"What did you get?" Henry asked as she pulled out the last packet of seeds.

Finley flipped it over and looked at the picture on the front. Her heart sank. "Radishes."

"Radishes are rad!" Henry said. He grabbed the packet as Finley slid into her seat. "They're spicy

and crunchy, and it says here they'll germinate in three days. I bet they'll be the first seeds to sprout!"

"Ooh," Olivia said, pointing to the picture on the packet. "Some of them are kind of purple."

Finley forced a smile. "I guess they're not so bad."

"Not so bad?" Henry shook his head. "They're Fin-tastic! We'll have radish salad, fried radishes, radish tacos —"

Olivia's eyes lit up. "What about those cute, little radish tea sandwiches?"

"We could make radish roses for a garnish," Finley said, brightening.

Ms. Bird rang the chime. "Now comes the fun part! When your group is ready, open your packet and pour half of the seeds into a cup. Then grab your journals and some clipboards from my desk, and bring everything outside."

"I'll copy the planting chart into my journal and fill it out," Finley offered.

"Hurry," Henry said. "I want to get my favorite trowel."

"Me too," Olivia said. "I need one that matches my gloves."

"Go ahead," Finley said. "I'll bring the seeds out when I'm done."

"Good idea — divide and conquer!" Henry grabbed his journal and a pencil and went to get a clipboard. Olivia followed, tugging on her gardening gloves.

Finley took out a pencil and copied the chart off the board, filling it in with the information from the back of the seed packet. When she'd finished, she poured some seeds into a cup and headed to Ms. Bird's desk for a clipboard. She'd just grabbed one when Will walked up.

"Radishes, huh?" he said, setting his cup down beside hers.

"Yep." Finley slid her journal under the clip on the clipboard.

Will raised an eyebrow. "Have you ever eaten one?" he asked.

"No," Finley answered. "But Henry likes them. And they only take three days to germinate. I bet they'll be the first crop we get to taste."

Will made a face. "If anybody wants to eat them."

"*I* want to eat them," Finley said, her cheeks getting hot. "It's good to try something new — if you're brave enough. And we're going to have the best radishes ever."

With that, she picked up the seed cup and marched out to the garden, where Henry and Olivia were waiting.

"What's wrong?" Henry asked. "You look mad."

"Will says no one will eat our radishes," Finley said. "I bet he hasn't even tried one."

"He doesn't know what he's missing," Henry said, taking the cup of seeds.

Olivia nodded. "Wait till he sees how pretty they are."

Finley hoped her friends were right. She checked the planting chart. "It says we should plant them in a row about half an inch deep and one inch apart. Let's get started. The sooner we plant them, the sooner they'll sprout."

The three of them got to work, setting up a seed assembly line. Finley poked a row of holes, Henry dropped a seed into each one, and Olivia followed and covered them with soil.

"This is fun," Olivia said as they planted. "The earth is soft, and it smells kind of good too."

"Rock-a-bye, radishes, cozy and snug . . ." Finley sang.

"Send up some shoots, and we'll give you a hug!" Henry finished.

Olivia laughed. "That makes no sense."

"Lullabies never do," Henry said. *"When the bough breaks, the cradle will fall, and down will come baby, cradle and all?* I mean, what's a cradle doing way up in a tree in the first place? And why would you sing that to a baby? It's terrifying."

Finley shrugged. "At least the baby has no idea what you're saying."

Olivia pinched one of the leftover seeds between her fingers. "I really hope this works. It doesn't seem like this tiny, dried-up speck could grow into a plant."

"Seeds grow all the time," Henry said. "We couldn't live without them."

Finley checked her planting chart. "In three days we should see some sprouts," she said, looking at her watch and writing down the time.

"Now we just water and wait," Henry said.

Finley pulled the hose over and filled the watering can so she could give the seeds a gentle shower. Then she bent down close to the ground.

"Okay, radishes," she whispered, "ready, set, grow!"

Chapter 8

THE NEEDS OF SEEDS

At recess, Finley took her journal out to the garden. Ms. Bird had said they should observe their beds carefully and write and draw what they see.

There's not much to see, Finley thought, crouching down to look closer. She sketched a gray square and wrote *plain old soil* under it with the date. Then she got out her music player and headphones and dangled them over the garden.

Henry flopped down on the grass beside her. "What's up?" he asked.

"I read in your mom's gardening magazine that some people think that plants grow better with classical music. So I'm playing my classical playlist for our seeds. Right now it's Vivaldi's 'Spring.' I thought that might inspire them. Next up, Mozart."

"I wonder if they like Elvis," Henry said, jumping up. "I'll be right *Bach*. I'm going to get my journal to make a *Liszt* of composers. I love *Liszts*."

Finley rolled her eyes. "Your music jokes are *classics*."

Just then Will walked by. "What are you doing?" he asked.

"Playing some classical music for our radishes," Finley said. "We want them to have good *taste*."

"Ha," Will said. "At least they'll have *good taste* even if they don't *taste good*."

"They'll taste great," Finley said. "I read that some early American colonists even ate radishes for breakfast."

Will wrinkled his nose. "I'll stick to cereal."

Finley shrugged. "Fine. That just means there'll be more for us."

* * *

After recess Ms. Bird called everyone inside. "We can't see much happening in our garden yet, but let's talk about what's going on underground. A lot of seeds wake up and germinate in the spring. What might cause them to do that?"

"Sunshine?" Henry guessed. "Warm weather?"

Ms. Bird nodded. "The days get longer in the spring, which means more direct sun and warmer soil. What else?"

"It rains a lot in spring," Finley said.

"Water is important for germination," Ms. Bird agreed. "Seeds also need oxygen. And some need light." She turned on the projector, and a picture of a seed appeared on the board. "This is a short video of a seed germinating. The first part of the plant that comes out of the protective seed coat is a special root called a radicle."

"Wow!" Finley and Henry said together as the video started and the outer layer of the seed split open. A tiny root pushed out and grew down into the soil.

"Next, the shoot pushes up," Ms. Bird continued.

As Finley watched, the root thickened. Then a little shoot emerged, wriggling out of the seed and raising its head above the ground.

"Ooh," Finley said softly. "It's magic."

"Of course, this video is sped up," Ms. Bird explained. "The process takes a lot longer in real life. And some seeds germinate faster than others."

As the shoot grew, the seed split open further. Two small leaves lifted out and opened up like an umbrella.

"The first leaves that many vegetables grow are called seed leaves," Ms. Bird said. "They look different from the leaves that grow later."

The class watched as more leaves appeared, and the plant grew taller, reaching for the sun.

"It looks like it's alive!" Will exclaimed.

"It's *ALIIIIIIVE!*" Henry said in his best Dr. Frankenstein voice.

"It *is* alive," Ms. Bird said. "Seeds are living things. Each one contains what's necessary to grow a new plant. And soon *your* seeds will be sprouting."

* * *

When the afternoon bell rang, Finley packed up her things and headed out to the garden.

"Where are you going?" Henry asked.

"To say goodbye to our seeds," Finley said.

Henry and Olivia followed her outside.

"I don't want to leave them," Finley said, bending down to inspect the earth. "They're so small and helpless. What if something happens to them?"

"They'll be fine," Olivia said. "They're safe and sound underground."

Henry nodded. "Our seeds have everything they need. It's even supposed to rain this weekend. When we see them on Monday, they'll be sprouts!"

Finley brightened. "You're right. Two, four, six, eight!" she cheered. "Come on, seeds, let's germinate!"

Chapter 9

FINLEY, FINLEY, SO CONTRARY

On Monday morning, Finley ran up the school steps. "Today's the day!" she announced to Henry as she bounded into class. "It's been three days since we planted our seeds. Get ready to meet our radishes!" She plunked down her backpack and ran to the window.

"See anything?" Henry asked, peering over her shoulder.

Finley shook her head. "Not yet. But I guess it hasn't been *exactly* three days." She glanced at the clock, then took out her journal and flipped to the planting table. "We planted the seeds at 8:56 a.m. on Friday, so we still have almost an hour."

All through math, Finley tried to focus, but she kept wondering if the seeds had sprouted. When the clock read 8:55, she held onto her chair so she wouldn't jump out of it to go look.

As soon as it was break time, she grabbed her journal and pencil and headed outside. But the garden looked the same — big, brown, and blank.

Finley sat on the grass and flipped to a new page in her journal. A minute later, Henry ambled over and flopped down beside her.

"What are you drawing?" he asked, taking a bite of his granola bar.

"Nothing," Finley said, shading in a square patch of gray. "Because there's nothing there."

"Our seeds are there," Henry reminded her. "They're under the earth, just waiting to sprout."

"Well, what are they waiting for?" Finley put down her journal and grabbed the watering can. "It's time. I told Zack and Evie I'd draw a picture of what the sprouts look like so they could see."

"Maybe they don't always take *exactly* three days," Henry said. "Maybe our seeds are running a little late."

Finley sighed. Then she dragged the hose over and filled up the watering can. As she finished watering, Olivia came outside.

"I think our seeds might be broken," Olivia said as she watched the water sink into the earth.

Just then there was a yell from the next bed over. "Hey!" Will shouted. "Our seeds are sprouting!"

Finley ran over to look. Sure enough, Will, Kate, and Lia's garden was dotted with tiny green specks.

"I thought *ours* were supposed to germinate first."
Finley pouted. "It's not fair."

"Looks like our carrots *beet* your radishes," Will
said. "Get it — *beet*?"

"We get it," Finley said. "We just don't *carrot* all."

Will grinned. "Maybe they'll come up soon. I'm
*root*ing for them!"

"Rrrr . . ." Finley glared as Will walked away.

"No need to growl," Henry said. "He's just joking."

Finley frowned. "I don't think it's funny."

"Don't worry," Olivia told her. "Our radishes will come up when they're ready."

"Gardening isn't a race," Henry added. "Maybe they'll taste better if they take their time."

Finley smiled. Her friends always knew what to say. "You're right," she said. "We're still going to have the best radishes ever. And I'm sure they'll be popping up any minute."

* * *

"Finley, Finley, so contrary, how does your garden grow?" Zack asked as Finley rummaged through the fridge looking for a snack after school.

Finley rolled her eyes. "Fine."

"Are we going to have a bumper crop of radishes?" Zack asked. "Because I'm ready for radish pizza, radish pancakes, radish ice cream . . ."

"Well, you'll just have to wait," Finley snapped. She grabbed some yogurt and a spoon and marched upstairs.

"What's the matter?" Zack called after her. "Was it something I said?"

Finley closed her bedroom door and flopped onto her bed. Then she opened her binder and flipped to the planting chart.

Germination time: three days, she read silently. *Where did we go wrong?*

Just then there was a knock on the door, and Zack poked his head in. "Hey," he said. "What's up?"

"Nothing."

"What's that?" Zack asked, pointing to the chart.

Finley sighed. "A planting chart for our radishes."

Zack studied the chart. "It says they only take three days to germinate. Didn't you plant them last week?"

Finley frowned. "Yeah."

"Maybe it's time for Plan B — a trip to the grocery store," Zack said. "We'll buy a bunch of fully grown radishes and go plant them in your garden. Problem solved."

"Problem *not* solved," Finley said. "Everyone would know. Radishes aren't big when they first come up — they're just tiny sprouts. Besides, the whole point is to grow them ourselves, not buy them."

"Okay," Zack said. "But let me know if you change your mind. It might be fun. We'd be like radish ninjas."

"Thanks," Finley said, "but I'll stick with Plan A. I'm sure our seeds will be sprouting soon. Get ready to taste the most Fin-tastic radishes ever."

"Suit yourself." Zack shrugged and slipped out the door.

I'm counting on you, radishes, Finley thought. *Don't prove me wrong.*

Chapter 10
THEY'RE ONLY SLEEPING

Two more days passed, and the garden was still bare.

After independent reading, Finley, Henry, and Olivia put their books away and stood at the window.

"This is ridiculous," Finley said. "Those seeds *have* to sprout soon."

Will squeezed in beside them and peered out at the garden. "I dunno. I think they might be dead."

"They're not dead," Henry said. "They're only sleeping."

"How do you know?" Will asked.

Henry grinned. "Because they're in a garden *bed*."

"We have to wake them up," Finley said. "Anybody got an alarm clock?"

"We don't need one," Henry said. "They have a built-in alarm."

Olivia crinkled her brow. "Well, what makes it go off? There's got to be *something* we can do to wake them up."

Just then Ms. Bird rang the chime. "Time for recess," she announced.

Finley, Henry, Olivia, and Will went to get their jackets.

"Want to play foursquare?" Henry asked.

"Sure," Finley said, pulling a crumpled paper out of her cubby. "Whoops — I forgot to turn in my homework. I'll be there in a minute."

"We'll get the ball," Olivia offered. "Meet you outside."

Finley set her homework on Ms. Bird's desk then slipped out the door, shivering as the brisk air greeted her. Zipping up her jacket, she felt the tingly tickle of an idea seed sprouting.

What if our seeds are chilly too? she thought. *If the soil isn't warm enough, maybe I should warm it up!*

Finley raced to the garden, tugged her jacket off, and spread it on the earth. Then she ran to catch up with the others.

"Where's your jacket?" Henry asked. "It's cold out here."

"It is a little chilly," Finley said. "I thought our seeds might be cold too, so I let them borrow it."

"You tucked them in?" Will asked, fighting back a grin.

"Why not?" Finley said. "They're in a garden *bed*, like Henry said. Now they'll be all snuggly warm."

"Did it say to do that on the package?" Henry asked.

"No," Finley said.

Olivia got her hard-thinking face. "Didn't Ms. Bird say that some seeds need light to germinate?"

Finley frowned. "Fiddlesticks. Now they'll never sprout."

"Sure they will," Henry said. "Just take the jacket off."

Finley ran to the garden and picked up her jacket. "Sorry about that," she whispered to the seeds. "I'll make it up to you."

* * *

The next day Finley got to school extra early and went straight out to the garden. Digging around in her backpack, she pulled out a flashlight and switched it on. Then she swept the beam back and forth, making sure to shine the light on every spot of soil.

"Rise and shine, little seeds!" she said in her cheeriest voice.

"What are you doing?" Will asked from behind her.

Finley jumped. "Trying not to scream. Quit sneaking up on me."

"Sorry," Will said. "I didn't mean to. What's with the flashlight? It's daytime."

"I'm helping our seeds catch up on their light," Finley explained. "Ms. Bird said some seeds need light to germinate."

"I don't know if that includes radishes," Will said. "Plus, that's not the right light. Plants need *sun*light."

"Well, I can't control the weather." Finley pointed to the clouds. "A flashlight's going to have to do." As she showered the garden with light, she pictured the seeds curled up under the soil, waiting to grow.

What are they waiting for? she thought. *What else did Ms. Bird say seeds need?* Then she remembered. *Oxygen!*

Finley crouched next to the garden and set the flashlight down. Taking a big breath, she blew on the soil. As she exhaled, she pictured the seeds waking up and stretching, just like the ones on the video Ms. Bird had shown in class.

"What are you doing *now*?" Will peered over her shoulder.

"Ms. Bird said seeds need oxygen," Finley said. "So I'm blowing on the soil to get more in there."

"You know there's more oxygen in the air we breathe *in* than in the air we breathe out, right?"

"I know," Finley said. "But every little bit helps."

Will grinned. "You might not be the best gardener, but you're definitely the most creative. I'm going to take care of my carrots."

Finley glared as Will walked away. Then she took an extra big breath. She was feeling a bit light-headed when Henry sat down next to her with his journal.

"You look a little funny," he said. "Are you okay?"

"I'm fine," Finley said. "I'm just trying to blow some oxygen into the soil for our seeds."

Henry raised his eyebrows. "I'm not so sure that's going to work."

Finley sat back on her heels. "Maybe we should just give up. We've tried everything, and they're not sprouting."

Henry shook his head. "We planted them in good soil, and we've been watering them carefully. All we have to do now is leave them alone and let them do their thing."

"But they're *not* doing their thing," Finley snapped. "That's the problem. And I'm all out of ideas."

With that, she grabbed her flashlight, struggled to her feet, and marched inside. *So much for being a Fin-tastic gardener,* Finley thought. *I can't even grow a single radish.*

Chapter 11
A LITTLE GREEN

Finley, Henry, and Olivia checked the garden when they got to school each morning, before they left each afternoon, and every chance in between. It had been two weeks since they'd planted their seeds, and all the other groups' seedlings were growing strong. Ms. Bird kept telling Finley to have patience, but patience wasn't one of Finley's strengths.

This morning wasn't any different. When Finley got to school, she went straight out to the garden. It looked the same as always — dark and still.

As Finley stared at the soil, Henry and Will ambled over. "Anything?" Henry asked.

"Nope," Finley said glumly. "I guess I really don't have a green thumb."

"We'll share our carrots with you," Will offered as he headed inside. "We've got plenty. And they'll probably be extra big since they came up early."

"It's my fault," Finley told Henry after Will had gone. "I must have my mom's bad gardening luck."

"There's no such thing," Henry said. "We've been taking good care of our seeds, so they'll grow. And if they don't, we'll still have lots of veggies to share."

Easy for you to say, Finley thought. *You didn't promise everyone the best radishes ever.*

Finley sighed. There was no point watching when nothing was growing. She swung her backpack onto her shoulder, and her favorite pencil fell out and into the garden. As she bent down to pick it up, something caught her eye. On the far side of the bed, if she looked at just the right angle, she could see a tiny speck of green.

Finley drew in her breath and scrambled around the garden. *Could it be? No. It's a piece of grass. But it doesn't look like grass. . . .* She leaned in closer.

"What are you looking at?" Henry asked.

"That little bit of green," Finley whispered.

"Where?" Olivia said, coming over to look.

"Right . . . there." Finley held her finger over the speck.

"Oooh!" Olivia reached toward it.

"Don't touch it!" Finley batted Olivia's hand away. "Sprouts are fragile. We don't want to hurt it."

"*My hand* is fragile," Olivia said. "We don't want to hurt it either."

"I think I see another one!" Henry pointed to the middle of the bed. "Rah, rah, radishes!"

"Come on!" Finley shrieked. "Let's tell Ms. Bird!"

Finley, Henry, and Olivia raced inside.

"Ms. Bird!" Finley said. "Our seeds have sprouted!"

Ms. Bird's eyes lit up. "Is that right?"

Finley nodded. "Come on — we'll show you!"
She dashed outside with Henry, Olivia, and Ms. Bird
close behind.

"See?" Finley pointed to the green speck. "And
there's one over there too."

Ms. Bird smiled. "They're beautiful!"

"I think they've gotten bigger already!" Olivia said
excitedly.

Henry looked at Finley and grinned. "I told you
they were only sleeping."

Ms. Bird got her camera from her desk and took
some pictures of the specks. "You should write down
the time so you can record their growth."

Henry grabbed his garden journal and a ruler.
"I've got it," he said. He quickly drew a growth
chart with *day* and *time* on the top and *centimeters*
on the side.

"Maybe we should measure in millimeters," Finley suggested, holding the ruler just behind one of the tiny sprouts. "Right now, they're barely one millimeter tall."

Ms. Bird smiled. "See? They came up right on time."

"Right on time?" Finley said. "I think they were a little late."

Ms. Bird shook her head. "No. But you might have to wait a while before you can harvest them."

"Why?" Finley asked. "Radishes are quick to grow."

"Radishes do grow fast," Ms. Bird said. "But these are carrots."

"Carrots?" Henry said. "We planted radishes."

Ms. Bird bent down and inspected the sprouts. "Nope. Carrots have long, thin seed leaves, like these. Radish sprouts have smooth, heart-shaped seed leaves." She pointed to the garden bed where Will, Kate, and Lia's sprouts grew in dotted rows. "Like those."

Finley's mouth hung open. *That's why theirs came up first!* She raced inside and marched over to Will's desk. "You stole our radishes!"

Will made a face. "Why would I do that?"

"I don't know," Finley said. "But you did. That's why your seeds sprouted so fast. They weren't carrot seeds at all."

Will frowned. "They were too. We just took care of them really well. We're natural gardeners."

Finley crossed her arms. "How long were your carrots supposed to take to germinate?"

"The package said they could take two weeks or more," Kate chimed in.

Finley raised an eyebrow. "And they came up in three days?"

Just then Ms. Bird walked up with Henry and Olivia. "Will, yours are *definitely* radishes," she said. "Sorry. I thought you all knew what you were growing. Carrots and radishes are similar. They're both root vegetables — that means we eat the root of the plant — but their leaves are very different.

Radishes take three or four days to germinate, while carrots can take up to three weeks."

Suddenly, Will's eyes lit up. "Hey," he said, "remember when we were going out to plant our seeds? We both set our cups down on Ms. Bird's desk. I think you might have taken mine."

Finley glared at Will. "Are you saying *I* stole your carrots?"

"No," Will said. "But maybe they got mixed up. The cups looked the same, and we were both in a hurry to get outside."

Finley shrugged. "I guess it's possible."

"It doesn't matter who grew what as long as everything is growing," Ms. Bird said brightly. "We'll have plenty of radishes *and* carrots."

"Sorry I accused you of stealing our radishes," Finley said after Ms. Bird had gone back to her desk.

"No worries," Will said. "Save a carrot for me?"

Finley nodded. "I'll trade you for a radish."

"Sure," Will said. "I might even taste one if you go first."

Finley grinned. "Deal."

Chapter 12

FLOWER POWER

While Finley and her friends waited for their carrots to grow, they helped plant a pollinator garden with zinnias, milkweed, and other bright flowers. Ms. Bird brought in pots full of blooming crocuses and grape hyacinths to welcome bees and butterflies.

Finley, Henry, and Olivia tended their garden carefully. They watered, weeded, and measured their carrots' growth every day. Soon the seedlings sent up tiny fans of feathery leaves.

"It's time to thin them," Ms. Bird announced. "That way each one will have enough room to grow healthy and strong. There should be one plant every two to three inches. You can pull out the rest of them to make some space. Tomorrow, we'll mulch between the rows."

Finley grabbed a carrot top and tugged gently. The tiny root slid out of the ground. "Look!" she said, dangling it in front of Henry's nose. "A carrot!"

Henry grinned. "A baby, baby, *baby* carrot!"

Finley, Henry, and Olivia went to work, thinning the seedlings until they were evenly spaced. As they were finishing up, Will came over to look.

"Wow," he said. "That's a lot of carrots."

Finley pulled one up and handed it to him. "Here," she said. "You can plant it with the radishes."

Will disappeared and came back minutes later with a radish seedling. "Trade," he said, holding it out.

"Thanks," Finley said, poking a deep hole in the soil with her finger and tucking it in.

"I'm glad we planted this garden for our service project," Will said. "At first I was hoping we could go to an assisted living center instead. My grandpa just moved to one, and he doesn't get many visitors. He had a big garden at his old house that I used to help him with." Will frowned and turned away. "But he can't garden anymore."

"I'm sorry," Finley said. "Maybe once our garden gets going, we could harvest some veggies and bring them to him."

Will looked at Finley and smiled. "He'd like that."

* * *

At lunchtime, Finley and Olivia spread out one of the picnic blankets Ms. Bird had brought in for the outdoor classroom. As they were taking out their lunches, Henry plunked down next to them. "It's a great day for a picnic."

"Perfect," Olivia said.

Finley surveyed the garden. "We need some stepping stones," she said. "We could make handprints on them to leave our mark when we move on to middle school."

"That would be fun," Olivia said. "Although, we've already left our mark." She gestured to the garden.

Finley took a deep breath. "Mmm. I love that garden-y smell."

"Check it out — flower power!" Henry pointed to one of the tiny grape hyacinths. A bee hovered over it then perched on the tight cluster of flowers.

"Ms. Bird, the flowers are working!" Finley called.

Ms. Bird came over to take a look. "Wow," she said. "Our first garden guest!"

"That's so cool!" Lia said.

Finley opened her lunch box and made herself a cheese-and-crackers sandwich. "I love eating outside. I'm glad we're here and not in there." She pointed to the cafeteria windows. "I just feel bad for the other classes."

Henry shrugged. "Think of it this way — because of you, Ms. Bird's fourth graders will be able to enjoy picnics at lunch for years to come."

Finley pictured Evie and her class eating under the trees and smiled. "Because of all of us," she said.

"Maybe it'll catch on and the other classes will make their own gardens," Olivia said, unpacking her lunch. "Then *all* of the students could have class outside and grow food for the cafeteria."

"If they build an outdoor pizza oven next year, I'm going to have to come back to fourth grade," Henry said.

Finley laughed. "We'll just have to build one in middle school. Since we already know how to make a garden, we could make one again."

"Remember Ms. Bird said we could have a harvest party?" Olivia asked. "We could serve veggies from the garden and give tours to the other classes and our families."

"I can't wait to show my family," Finley said. "Especially Zack. He didn't think we could grow anything."

Henry shook his head. "Well, he was wrong. This garden was one of the best idea seeds you've ever sprouted. Way to use your Flower Power."

Finley grinned. "Thanks." She glanced around the garden. "Remember the quote on the poster I read in class?"

"The one about being lost and found?" Olivia said.

Finley nodded. "I think it means that when you do things for other people, like our service project, you might find out something about yourself."

"Like I found out that I actually *like* digging in the dirt," Olivia said.

"*Soil*," Henry corrected.

"Right — *soil*." Olivia grinned.

"And I found out that just like a tiny seed, I can do big things." Henry pointed at the garden. Then he glanced at Finley. "What about you?"

"I found out that I can garden. And that sometimes I'm not very patient. But I'll keep

working on it — good stuff is worth waiting for."
Finley smiled at Henry and Olivia. "Thanks for
making the garden with me. You're good friends."

"Takes one to know one," Henry said.

Finley laughed. "Takes one to *grow* one."

About the Author

Jessica Young grew up in Ontario, Canada. The same things make her happy now as when she was a kid: dancing, painting, music, digging in the dirt, picnics, reading, and writing. Like Finley Flowers, Jessica loves making stuff. When she was little, she wanted to be a tap-dancing flight attendant/veterinarian, but she's changed her mind! Jessica currently lives with her family in Nashville, Tennessee.

About the Illustrator

When Jessica Secheret was young, she had strange friends that were always with her: felt pens, colored pencils, brushes, and paint. After Jessica repainted all the walls in her house, her parents decided it was time for her to express her "talent" at an art school — the famous École Boulle in Paris. After several years at various architecture agencies, Jessica decided to give up squares, rulers, and compasses and dedicate her heart and soul to what she'd always loved — putting her own imagination on paper. Today, Jessica spends her time in her Paris studio, drawing for magazines and children's books in France and abroad.

Pollinator Puddle

Busy bees and butterflies need water. Create a pollinator puddle that's just the right size for your garden visitors.

What You'll Need:

- shallow flowerpot saucer or ceramic dish
- sand and gravel (no chemicals added)
- small rocks
- water

What to Do:

1. Fill your dish with sand or gravel and add water until it forms shallow puddles.
2. Place small rocks around the sand or gravel so bees and butterflies will have a place to land and drink.
3. Place the dish in a sunny spot next to pollinator-friendly flowers. Keep the sand or gravel moist, and wait to welcome thirsty pollinators!

Plant Markers

Where did we plant the lettuce? Are those beet or radish seedlings? Create some beautiful and handy garden markers to help you tell what's what. They make great gifts for gardeners too.

What You'll Need:

- round or flat rocks (big enough and smooth enough to write on), wooden mixing spoons, or unused paint stir sticks from the hardware store
- permanent, non-toxic paint markers or chalk markers

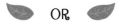 OR

- thin wire and alphabet beads

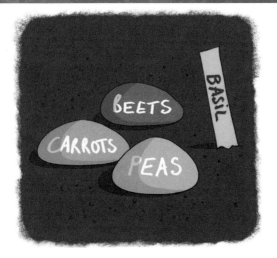

What to Do:

1. Using paint or chalk markers, write the names of plants across the rocks or the insides of wooden spoons. Decorate with painted borders, pictures of plants, or other small designs.

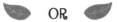 OR

1. String alphabet beads onto wire to spell out plant names, then bend the wire down on each side to hold the beads in place. Twist the ends of the wire together to make a long stake to stick into the soil.
2. Stick your plant markers into the garden soil to mark where you've planted different types of seeds.

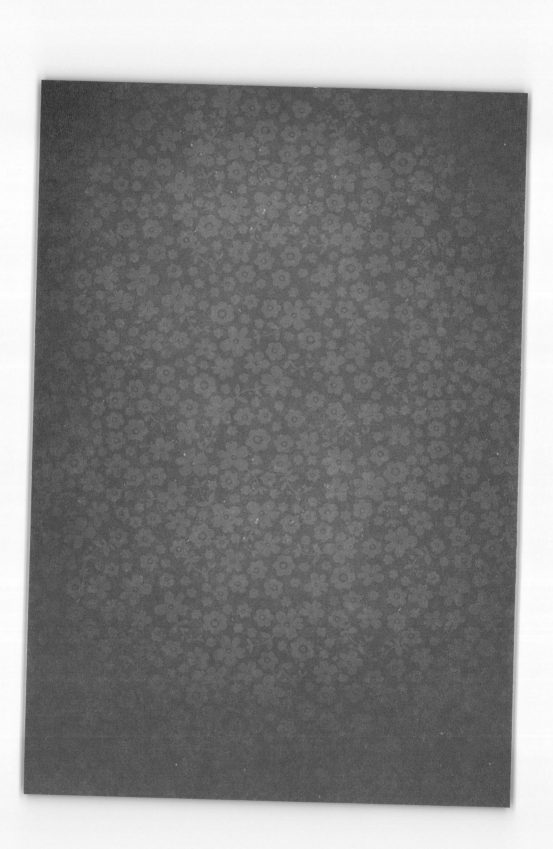